KT-174-546

BAINTE DEN STOC

WITHDRAWN FROM
DÚN LAOGHAIRE-RATHDOWN COUNTY
LIBRARY STOCK

Our Castle

First published in 2010
by Wayland

Text copyright © Annemarie Young
Illustration copyright © Louise Redshaw

Wayland
338 Euston Road
London NW1 3BH

Wayland Australia
Level 17/207 Kent Street
Sydney, NSW 2000

The rights of Annemarie Young to be identified as the Author and
Louise Redshaw to be identified as the Illustrator of this Work have been
asserted by them in accordance with the Copyright, Designs and Patents Act, 1988.

All rights reserved

Series Editor: Louise John
Editor: Katie Powell
Cover design: Paul Cherrill
Design: D.R.ink
Consultant: Shirley Bickler

A CIP catalogue record for this book is available from the British Library.

ISBN 9780750260411

Printed in China

Wayland is a division of Hachette Children's Books,
an Hachette UK Company

www.hachette.co.uk

Our Castle

Written by Annemarie Young
Illustrated by Louise Redshaw

WAYLAND

We got a spade
for our castle.

We got a bucket
for our castle.

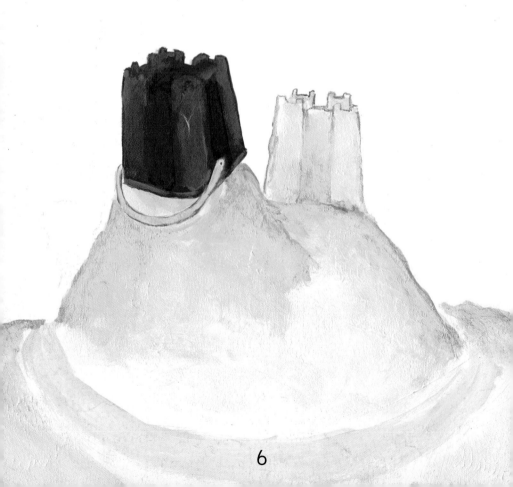

We got a shell
for our castle.

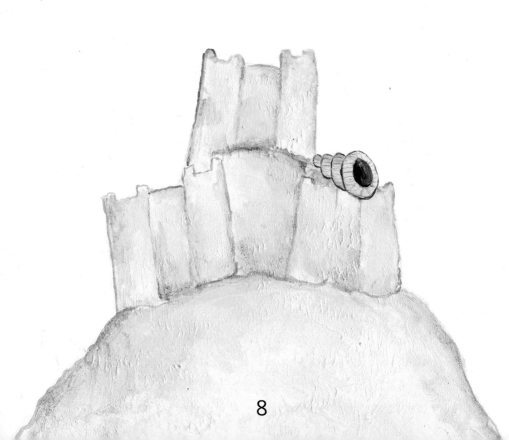

We got a rock
for our castle.

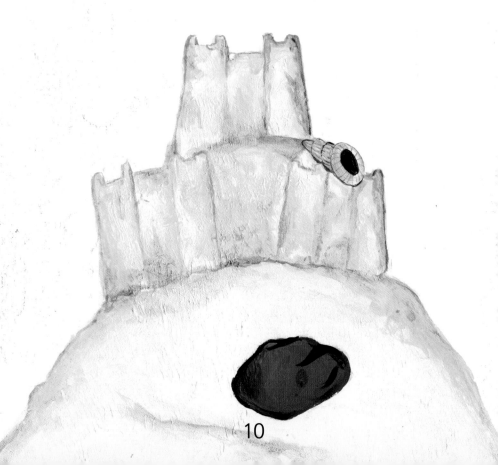

We got a starfish
for our castle.

We got a stick
for our castle.

We got a feather
for our castle.

We got a flag
for our castle.

19

Oh no!

21

Guiding a First Read of
Our Castle

It is important to talk through the book with the child before they read it alone. This prepares them for the way the story unfolds, and allows them to enjoy the pictures as you both talk naturally, using the language they will later encounter when reading. Read the brief overview below, and then follow the suggestions:

1. Talking through the book
   When the family went to the beach, they made a sand castle. The children tell us what they got for their castle.

   Let's read the title: **Our Castle**
   Turn to page 4. The children said,
   "We got a spade for our castle."
   On the next page they got a bucket.
   "We got a bucket for our castle."
   And what did they get on page 8?

Continue through the book, guiding the discussion to fit the text as the child looks at the illustrations.

   What happened on page 18?
   Oh no! The waves are washing
   the castle away.

2. A first reading of the book

Ask the child to read the book independently, pointing carefully under each word (tracking), while thinking about the story. Praise attempts by the child to correct themselves, and prompt them to use their letter knowledge, the punctuation and check the meaning, for example:

> **Did your pointing fit? No? Let's try again, and keep your finger on 'starfish' while you read it. It's all one word. Well done.**
>
> **Yes, 'twig' makes sense. What sound does 'twig' start with? Read it again and check if that word starts with 't'. What else could it be? Is 'stick' right? Good checking.**

3. Follow-up activities

The high frequency words in this title are:

a   for   got   we

Leabharlanna Dhún Laoghaire · h An Dúin

· Select a new high frequency word, and ask the child or group to find it throughout the book. Discuss the shape of the letters and the letter sounds.
· To memorise the word, ask the child to write it in the air, then write it repeatedly on a whiteboard or on paper, leaving a space between each attempt.

4. Encourage

· Reading the book again – with expression.
· Drawing a picture based on the story.
· Writing one or two sentences using the practised word.

START READING is a series of highly enjoyable books for beginner readers. **The books have been carefully graded to match the Book Bands widely used in schools.** This enables readers to be sure they choose books that match their own reading ability.

Look out for the Band colour on the book in our Start Reading logo.

The Bands are:

Pink Band 1A & 1B

Red Band 2

Yellow Band 3

Blue Band 4

Green Band 5

Orange Band 6

Turquoise Band 7

Purple Band 8

Gold Band 9

START READING books can be read independently or shared with an adult. They promote the enjoyment of reading through satisfying stories supported by fun illustrations.

Annemarie Young lives in Cambridge but grew up in a city by the sea. She and her family like going for walks whatever the weather, building sand castles and finding all sorts of bugs in the garden.

Louise Redshaw likes to go for long walks and eat picnic lunches with friends when she's not too busy drawing. She loves animals but likes donkeys the most and one day wants to have a huge garden where she can keep her own donkey.